T0197475

Our Princess

ANN BARTHOLOMEW SCHMIDT

Copyright © 2022 by Ann Bartholomew Schmidt. 841119

All rights reserved. No part of this book may be reproduced or
transmitted in any form or by any means, electronic or mechanical,
including photocopying, recording, or by any information storage
and retrieval system, without permission in writing from the
copyright owner.

This is a work of fiction. Names, characters, places and incidents
either are the product of the author's imagination or are used
fictitiously, and any resemblance to any actual persons, living or
dead, events, or locales is entirely coincidental.

To order additional copies of this book, contact:
Xlibris
844-714-8691
www.Xlibris.com
Orders@Xlibris.com

ISBN: Softcover   978-1-6698-2299-8
          EBook   978-1-6698-2298-1

Print information available on the last page

Rev. date: 04/28/2022

Our
Princess

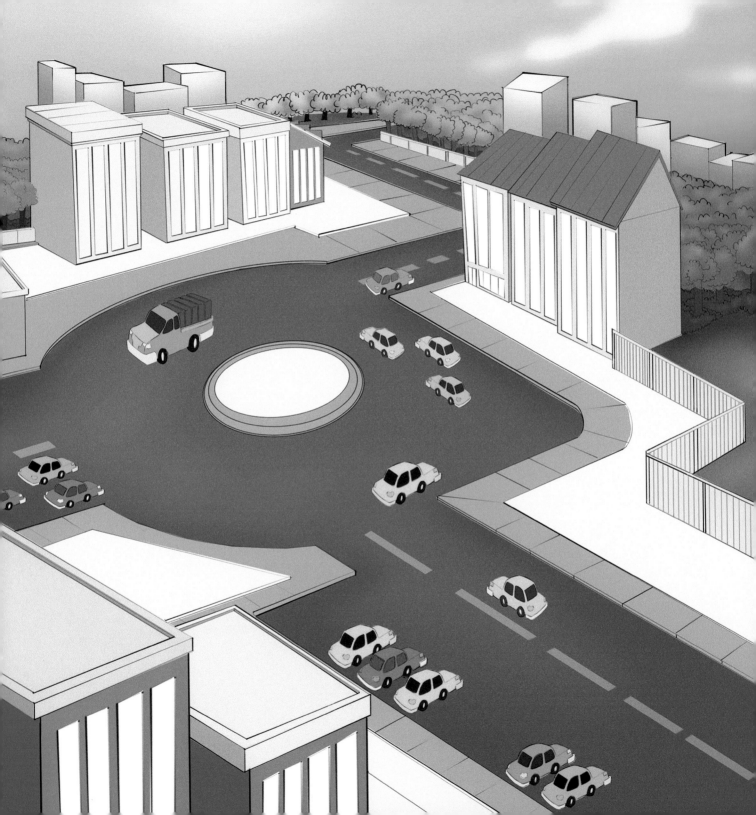

We have a princess in our town
Her coach is silver blue.
We like to stand outside our house
As she is passing through

Thursday is the day she comes
And stops beside our drive.
Mom and I wait patiently
For our princess to arrive.

She is, oh, just beautiful!
Her hair is cocoa brown.
She wears it in a hundred braids
That form a sparkling crown.

Her work is so important.
She cannot stop to play.
And I often feel a little sad
To see her ride away.

Her driver is a friendly man.
He always waves to me.
But he is serious about his job
Transporting royalty.

Mom and I both smile
As she gives her regal nod,
And when she steps up to her coach
The two of us applaud!

Our town has a princess.
She is very strong and brave.
And I feel extra special
When our princess stops to wave!

Printed in the United States
by Baker & Taylor Publisher Services